ALBERT PUJOLS

BY ALEX MONNIG

Published by ABDO Publishing Company, PO Box 398166, Minneapolis, MN 55439.
Copyright © 2012 by Abdo Consulting Group, Inc. International copyrights reserved in all
countries. No part of this book may be reproduced in any form without written permission
from the publisher. SportsZone™ is a trademark and logo of ABDO Publishing Company.

Printed in the United States of America,
North Mankato, Minnesota
092011
012012

Editor: Chrös McDougall
Copy Editor: Anna Comstock
Series Design: Craig Hinton
Cover and Interior Production: Kazuko Collins

Photo Credits: Richard Drew/AP Images, cover, 1; Eric Gay/AP Images, 4; Tom Gannam/
AP Images, 6, 9, 13, 17, 21; Diamond Images/Getty Images, 10; Robert F. Bukaty/
AP Images, 15; James A. Finley/AP Images, 18; Elise Amendola/AP Images, 23; Jeff
Roberson/AP Images, 24, 29; David J. Phillip/AP Images, 26

Library of Congress Cataloging-in-Publication Data
Monnig, Alex.
  Albert Pujols : groundbreaking slugger / by Alex Monnig.
      p. cm. — (Playmakers)
  Includes bibliographical references and index.
  ISBN 978-1-61783-294-9
  1. Pujols, Albert, 1980—Juvenile literature. 2. Hispanic American baseball players—
Biography—Juvenile literature. I. Title.
  GV865.P85M67 2012
  796.357092—dc23
  [B]
                                    2011038900

TABLE OF CONTENTS

Albert Pujols

CHAPTER 1

A LONG WAY FROM HOME

It was Game 3 of the 2011 World Series. The National League (NL) champion St. Louis Cardinals and the American League champion Texas Rangers were tied at one game apiece. The first team to win four games would be Major League Baseball (MLB) champions.

Cardinals slugger Albert Pujols started Game 3 with two singles in his first three at-bats. He was just getting started. Pujols hit home runs in the sixth,

Albert Pujols blasts one of his three home runs in Game 3 of the 2011 World Series.

Albert has won two Gold Glove Awards through 2011. That meant he was the best fielding first baseman in the NL those years.

seventh, and ninth innings. That made him 5-for-6 on the night with six runs batted in (RBIs). Only two other players had ever homered three times in a World Series game. One of them was Babe Ruth. The Cardinals won easily, 16–7.

Cardinals fans were used to Albert's heroics by 2011. He had been one of the most feared hitters in all of baseball for more than a decade. Everything seemed to come easy to him on the field. It was not always that way, though.

Albert was born on January 16, 1980, in Santo Domingo, Dominican Republic. His full name is José Alberto Pujols Alcántara. Baseball and softball are big parts of Dominican culture. So Albert was introduced to the sports at a very young age.

Albert's father is named Bienvenido. And he was Albert's hero growing up. Bienvenido was a popular softball pitcher in the Dominican Republic. Albert often wore his father's softball jerseys at home. But Albert's parents were not always around to care for him. Instead, Albert's grandmother, America, took care of him.

Albert lived with America and her 10 children. He was the youngest in the house. His aunts and uncles were more like his brothers and sisters. Sometimes it was hard for the poor family. But that did not stop Albert from playing baseball. He used sticks as bats. For gloves, he used empty cardboard milk

Julio Franco was Albert's baseball hero when he was growing up. Franco was an infielder from the Dominican Republic. He played for eight major league teams during a 23-year career.

cartons. Albert did not even have baseballs. So he used limes instead.

Albert and his dad moved to New York when Albert was 16. But America thought it was too dangerous there. So Albert and Bienvenido soon moved to Kansas City, Missouri.

Despite the moves, Albert never gave up baseball. He played shortstop for the Fort Osage High School team. That is where people began to learn about his talent. Albert was hitting balls much farther than the other boys. The slugger was named to the All-State team. He even helped Fort Osage win a state title in his first season.

The move was not as easy off the baseball diamond. People in the Dominican Republic speak Spanish. Albert had trouble understanding and speaking English in his new home. He also got behind in his schoolwork.

Fans watching the Fort Osage baseball team got a preview of things to come at one 1998 game. Albert slugged a home run that crashed off an air conditioner high up a building that was almost 450 feet (137 m) away. That is considered a big home run even by MLB standards.

Albert has won six Silver Slugger Awards as the NL's top hitting first baseman through 2011.

But Albert did not give up. He worked hard on his baseball skills and his schoolwork. The hard work paid off. Albert had a .660 batting average during his second season, in 1998. And he had eight home runs. Albert was again named to the All-State team. And he earned enough high school credits to graduate.

Albert hoped to someday play in the major leagues. But he would have to change the minds of some doubters first.

10   *Albert Pujols*

CHAPTER 2

YOUNG STAR

Albert Pujols was a high school baseball star. But major league teams were not ready to draft him. So Pujols instead went to Maple Woods Community College in January 1999. The school is in Kansas City.

Pujols starred for the baseball team. He had a .461 batting average. And he added 22 home runs and 80 RBIs. That was enough to earn him a spot on the All-Region team.

Pujols played for the Potomac Cannons, one of the Cardinals' minor league teams, in 2000.

Even so, major league teams were still unsure about Pujols. He had shown that he could hit. But some scouts worried about his defense. He was a shortstop at the time. And he was still fairly small. Those concerns showed at the MLB Draft that summer. That is when MLB teams select amateur players. Teams chose more than 400 players before Pujols. The St. Louis Cardinals finally selected him in the 13th round.

Pujols was disappointed that so many teams had passed on him. He was also disappointed with the Cardinals' contract offer. So he played in a summer league for top college players in Kansas instead. The Cardinals made a new offer to Pujols after that. And this time he signed.

Around that same time, Pujols met a 21-year-old woman named Deidre. The two started dating. But Deidre was nervous. Her young daughter Isabella had Down syndrome. She worried

Pujols had a day to remember in his debut for Maple Woods. He hit a grand slam off future All-Star pitcher Mark Buehrle. Pujols also turned an unassisted triple play in the same game.

US Senator Claire McCaskill, *left*, presents Pujols and his wife Deidre, *center*, with an award for public service in 2010.

that Pujols would stop dating her if he found out. Instead, Pujols fell in love with Deidre. And he began to think of Isabella as his own daughter. Pujols and Deidre married in early 2000.

Pujols had signed with the Cardinals. But professional baseball players almost always begin in the minor leagues. Pujols followed that path. He quickly began rising to the top of the minors, though. Pujols began in Class A. That is the fourth division of baseball. But by the end of his first season, he was in Class AAA. That is the top league outside of the majors. He was even the Most Valuable Player (MVP) for his Class A team.

It was an exciting time for the Pujols family. Deidre and Pujols had their first child together after that season. They named him Alberto Jr. The excitement was just beginning.

The Cardinals invited Pujols to spring training in 2001. The team planned to have him start the season back in Class AAA. But Pujols made sure that did not happen. He played so well that the team had no choice but to bring him up to the majors. Pujols was the Cardinals' Opening Day left fielder.

Pujols went on to have one of the best rookie seasons ever. He hit .329, slugged 37 home runs, and had 130 RBIs. All three of those were team highs. Pujols was named to the NL All-Star team. He also won the NL Rookie of the Year Award and finished fourth in the NL MVP voting. Behind Pujols's powerful

Pujols is known for his consistency. That began during his rookie year in 2001. He made it on base in 48 straight games that year. The streak lasted from July 28 to September 22.

Pujols fields a grounder during spring training in 2004 while preparing to become the Cardinals' everyday first baseman.

bat, the Cardinals had just one losing season between 2001 and 2011. And they made the playoffs in five of his first six seasons.

One of the big concerns about Pujols in high school and college was his defense. The Cardinals were not sure where he fit best. Pujols played left field, right field, third base, and first base during his rookie season. He played mostly outfield until 2004. Then he became the Cardinals' first baseman.

The position changes on defense never affected his offense. Pujols again led the Cardinals in most major hitting categories in 2002. And this time he finished second in the NL MVP voting. The Cardinals returned to the playoffs for the third straight season. However, they fell just short of the World Series.

Few people had known of Pujols in 1999. But by 2002, he had proven that he was for real. And there was no slowing him down. Pujols hit a career-high .359 in 2003. He led the NL in hits, runs, batting average, and doubles. However, the Cardinals missed the playoffs for the first time since adding Pujols.

The 2004 season was different. The Cardinals won 105 games. That was the most of any team in baseball. And Pujols was a big reason for their success. He again led the Cardinals in most offensive categories. He was again an All-Star. And he finished third in the NL MVP voting.

Pujols played in 475 of the Cardinals' 486 regular-season games from 2001 to 2003. He suffered with a condition called plantar fasciitis in 2004. It caused him great pain in his heel. Still, Pujols played in 154 of the team's 162 games that year.

Pujols celebrates the Cardinals' 2004 NL pennant with the home fans at Busch Stadium.

The Cardinals stayed hot in the playoffs. They reached the World Series for the first time since 1987. Pujols hit .414 with six home runs and 14 RBIs in 15 postseason games. The Boston Red Sox swept the Cardinals in the World Series. But Pujols had shown he could play well on the biggest stage. All he had left to prove was that he could lead the Cardinals to the title.

Albert Pujols

CHAPTER 3

TO THE TOP

Albert Pujols had been moved when he first met Deidre's daughter, Isabella. He wanted to make a difference in her life and the lives of others affected by Down syndrome. So in 2005, Albert and Deidre started the Pujols Family Foundation.

The organization has two main goals. One is to teach people about Down syndrome while also donating money to those with the disease. The other

Pujols hit at least 32 home runs in each of his first 11 seasons. He hit more than 40 homers six times.

goal is to help children in need in the Dominican Republic. Pujols has remained very active in both causes.

He also remained active on the baseball diamond. The Cardinals won 100 games in 2005. That was more than any other team. Pujols was also one of the best in baseball that year. He hit .330 with 41 home runs and 117 RBIs. That was good enough to finally earn him the NL MVP Award. However, Pujols was more concerned with winning his first World Series.

St. Louis swept the San Diego Padres in the first round of the playoffs. Then the Cardinals met the Houston Astros in the second round. The two teams were division rivals. St. Louis was down to its last out in Game 5. Pujols hit a massive home run in the bottom of the ninth inning to keep the season alive. But it would only last one more game. The Cardinals lost. And Pujols's first World Series championship would have to wait.

Pujols's disappointment from missing the World Series was soon overtaken by joy. Deidre gave birth to the family's third

Pujols holds his daughter Sophia while talking with reporters. Family has always been important to Pujols.

child that year. Daughter Sophia was born in November. That capped off a busy year for Pujols and his family.

Pujols and the Cardinals returned in the spring of 2006 with confidence. They believed they had a chance to win the World Series. Pujols again shined. He made his fourth All-Star Game in as many years. But he also got injured. And he had to go on the disabled list for the first time.

The injury was not serious, though. Pujols came back and played very well. He had long been known for his great hitting. But in 2006, Pujols took home his first Gold Glove Award. Those are given to the top fielder at each position in each league. He had come a long way since his community college days.

Still, the Cardinals barely made the playoffs that year. But that hardly mattered once they were in. The team found new life

One of the most popular events the Pujols Family Foundation puts on is the Autumn Prom. It is a formal dance for people with Down syndrome. Albert and Deidre started the event in 2007. It has grown bigger each year. The two attend the dance every year. Pujols is known for dancing with many of the guests.

Pujols, with son Alberto Jr. on his shoulders, holds the World Series trophy with Cardinals manager Tony La Russa, *right*.

in the postseason. Pujols played well as the Cardinals beat the Padres and the New York Mets. Then they played the Detroit Tigers in the World Series.

The Tigers were able to slow down Pujols a bit. They did that by not giving him much to hit. Still, he had three hits and five walks in the World Series. He also scored three runs. And this time, the Cardinals won. They beat the Tigers four games to one. Pujols was finally a World Series champion!

Albert Pujols

CHAPTER 4

CONTINUED EXCELLENCE

Pujols is nicknamed "The Machine." That is because fans know they can expect him to always play at a high level. He is very consistent, just like a machine.

The 2007 season was one of Pujols's worst seasons. But it was a season most players could only dream of having. He hit .327 with 32 home runs and 103 RBIs. However, through 2011, it was the Cardinals' only losing season since Pujols joined the majors.

Pujols recorded at least a .300 batting average, 100 RBIs, and 30 home runs in each of his first ten seasons.

MLB commissioner Bud Selig, *right*, and Phil Caruso from Chevrolet, *left*, present Pujols with the Roberto Clemente Award in 2008.

Pujols came back strong. He batted .357 in 2008. Then he hit an NL-best 47 home runs and drove in 135 runs in 2009. The Cardinals' slugger was named the NL MVP both seasons. But again, the team struggled. St. Louis missed the playoffs in 2008 and was swept in the first round of the playoffs in 2009.

Pujols was playing great baseball. But perhaps the most noteworthy award he received during that time had nothing to do with his skills on the diamond. After each season, MLB gives out the Roberto Clemente Award. Clemente was a Pittsburgh

Albert and Deidre welcomed their fourth child, Ezra, to the world on February 5, 2010. Their other children are Isabella, Alberto Jr., and Sophia.

Pirates star during the 1960s and 1970s. He died while trying to deliver food and supplies to earthquake victims in Nicaragua. So the Roberto Clemente Award is given to the baseball player who is most active in the community.

MLB gave Pujols that award in 2008. The award honored his work with the Pujols Family Foundation. The foundation had already helped more than 500 families affected by Down syndrome in the St. Louis area. MLB also recognized Pujols's work with other organizations. Among them were the Boys & Girls Club of America and the Ronald McDonald House.

Pujols had already won the Rookie of the Year Award, the MVP Award three times, and a World Series championship. But he said the Roberto Clemente Award was the most meaningful. Pujols said he wanted to be remembered as much for his charity work as for his baseball success.

The Cardinals continued to be a winning team. Pujols led the NL in home runs, RBIs, and runs scored in 2010. He also finished second in MVP voting. But St. Louis missed the playoffs.

Pujols became the only player to hit at least .300 with 30 home runs and 100 RBIs in each of his first 10 MLB seasons. Pujols also placed in the top ten in MVP voting in each of those years. And he was selected for nine All-Star Games.

After ten very strong years, Pujols struggled a bit in 2011. He missed the All-Star Game for only the second time. His .299 batting average and 99 RBIs were career lows. To make matters worse, the Cardinals were 10.5 games out of the playoffs with just 31 games remaining.

Then the Cardinals got hot. They clinched a playoff berth in the last game of the season. Then they dispatched the favored Philadelphia Phillies and Milwaukee Brewers in the NL playoffs.

That set up the dramatic World Series against the Texas Rangers. Pujols had been hot during the playoffs. Then he cooled down in the World Series. He only had one hit outside of his big Game 3. Like in the 2006 World Series, the opposing pitchers did not give him many good pitches.

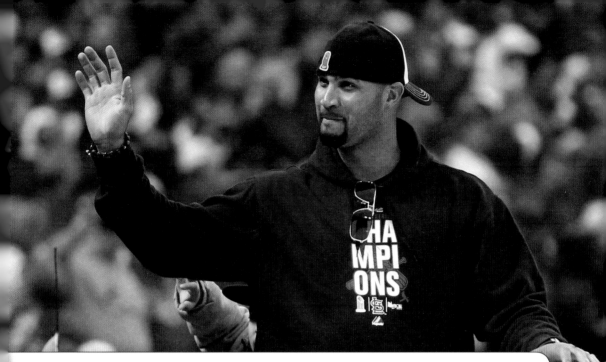

Pujols waves to fans during the Cardinals' 2011 World Series victory parade through downtown St. Louis.

The Cardinals were on the verge of losing the series in Game 6. Texas had a 7–5 lead with one out in the bottom of the ninth. Then Pujols ripped a double. It started a rally that tied the game. St. Louis finally won the game in 11 innings. That set up a deciding Game 7. The Cardinals won that too.

Pujols had come a long way since the disappointing 1999 MLB Draft. His first 10 seasons were unmatched in MLB history. And now he was a two-time World Series champion. Nothing can stop The Machine.

FUN FACTS AND QUOTES

- One of the reasons Albert Pujols keeps having so much success is because he keeps working hard. He said he takes between 15,000 and 20,000 practice swings every year.

- Every year, Pujols returns to Santo Domingo, Dominican Republic, with other members of the Pujols Family Foundation to help those in need. He delivers beds and organizes doctors to visit poor neighborhoods, called *batays*.

- In 2006, Pujols opened a restaurant called Pujols 5 in St. Louis. It is a sports bar where fans go to watch sports on the restaurant's numerous TVs.

- Albert and Deidre struggled with money before the Cardinals signed him. She worked three jobs. And he worked in a pizzeria and a country club when he was not playing in the minors. They were only able to spend $150 on their wedding.

- On February 7, 2007, Pujols officially became a citizen of the United States. He scored a perfect 100 on his citizenship test.

WEB LINKS

To learn more about Albert Pujols, visit ABDO Publishing Company online at **www.abdopublishing.com**. Web sites about Pujols are featured on our Book Links page. These links are routinely monitored and updated to provide the most current information available.

GLOSSARY

batting average
A percentage of how many hits a player has compared to how many times they bat.

charity
Money given or work done to help people in need.

contract
An agreement between a team and a player that determines the player's salary and length of commitment with that team.

debut
The first appearance.

Down syndrome
A condition that affects the brain's development.

draft
When MLB teams select players in high school and college to come play on their team.

minor leagues
Leagues made of developmental teams so players can practice and improve before playing in MLB.

postseason
The games in which the best teams play in after the regular season, including two rounds of playoffs and the World Series.

rookie
A player who is playing his first season in MLB.

scouts
People employed by baseball teams who watch other players to determine their strengths and weaknesses.

spring training
The time before the regular season when teams go to Florida or Arizona to prepare.

INDEX

FURTHER RESOURCES

Christopher, Matt. *On the Field With…Albert Pujols.* New York: Hachette Book
   Group, 2009.

Gitlin, Marty. *St. Louis Cardinals.* Edina, MN: ABDO Publishing Co., 2011.

Riach, Steve. *True Heroes of Sports: Discovering the Heart of a Champion.*
   Nashville, TN: Thomas Nelson, 2009.